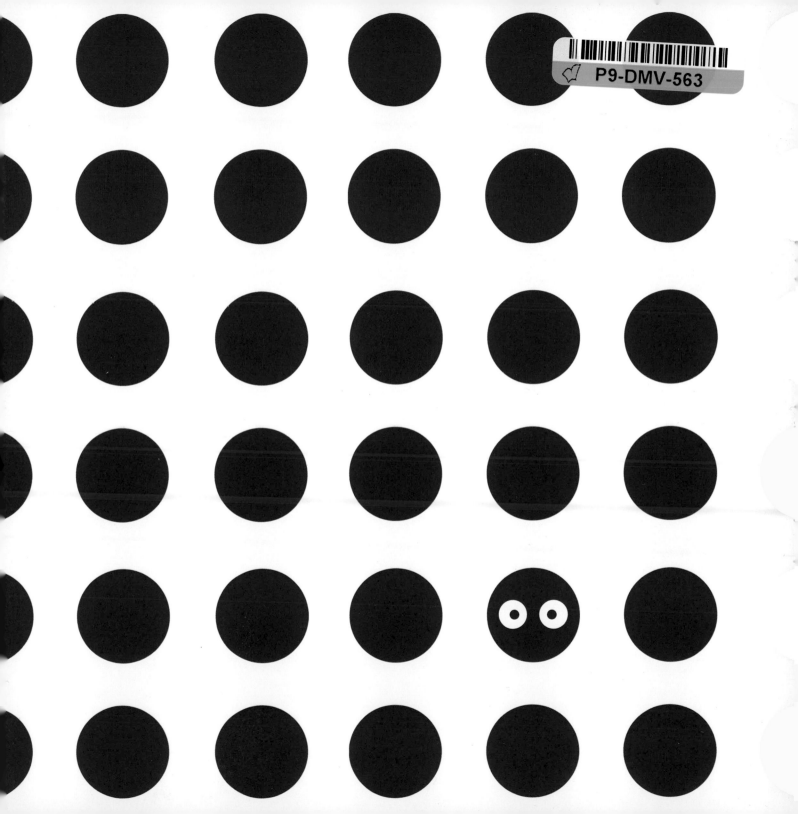

Not Just a DOT

Can you find Dot on this page?

To my family, who may be small in comparison to the Cosmos, but are everything to me.

Sky Pony Press books may be purchased in bulk at special discounts for sales promotion, corporate gifts, fund-raising, or educational purposes. Special editions can also be created to specifications. For details, contact the Special Sales Department, Sky Pony Press, 307 West 36th Street, 11th Floor, New York, NY 10018 or info@skyhorsepublishing.com.

Sky Pony® is a registered trademark of Skyhorse Publishing, Inc.®, a Delaware corporation.

Visit our website at www.skyponypress.com.

10 9 8 7 6 5 4 3 2 1

Manufactured in China, May 2014
This product conforms to CPSIA 2008

Library of Congress Cataloging-in-Publication Data is available on file.

Jacket art and design by Loryn Brantz

Print ISBN: 978-1-62914-622-5
Ebook ISBN: 978-1-63220-221-5

NOT JUST A

DOT

LORYN BRANTZ

Sky Pony Press
New York

This is Dot

Dot feels small and unimportant.

"I'm just a little ol' dot. Nobody needs me."

See, Dot? You're very **useful!**

"That's just one guy. Nobody else needs me."

He's not the only one who **needs** you.
This dalmatian looks like he's missing a dot!

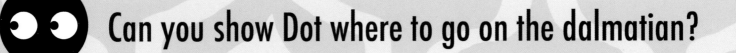 Can you show Dot where to go on the dalmatian?

You did it! **Good job.**

Now the dalmatian has all his dots!

I guess I am a little bit useful...

A little? You're much more than a **LITTLE** bit useful.

How can this little girl ask for ice cream without **you** on the **question mark?**

Can **YOU** show Dot where to go on the
question mark?

Very good!

Now she can enjoy her ice cream!

Wow, I guess I am kind of useful!

But I still feel **too** small.

That's just silly, Dot.
Look at these ants. They're small, just like you.

Now, if you take a step back, they look like **little** dots, too.

And if we get into this hot air balloon...

and go way up **high,**

eventually all those people
on the ground will just be dots.

And if we go even higher...

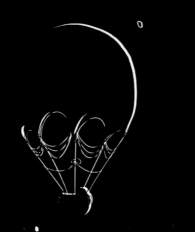

the **whole world,** and everything and everyone on it, will look like a dot, too.